Adoption Stories for Young Children

Written by Randall B. Hicks

Photographs by William H. Rockey

WORDSLINGER PRESS
Sun City, California

Dedicated to my children,
the best kids in the world!

Special thanks to the caring teachers of the Anne Sullivan Preschool for their assistance and cooperation, and to Sharon Kaplan Roszia for her title suggestion.

WordSlinger Press
P.O. Box 53
Sun City, CA 92506-9998
(909) 412-3788

ISBN: 0-9631638-2-5
Library of Congress Catalog Card Number: 95-061150

Printed and manufactured in the United States of America
Second Printing

Talking About Adoption with Your Child

Some adoptive parents feel very comfortable in discussing adoption with their child, while others have some anxiety. All adoptive parents, however, have one thing in common. They understand that not only does their child need and deserve knowledge of how their family was created through adoption, but also that his or her knowledge must be provided in a way which will give their child the pride and self-respect every person needs as a foundation in life.

What do you say and when do you say it? Every child—and family situation—is different, but there are many common themes which the adoption community has come to embrace. The practice followed by some parents many years ago of hiding any information about adoption until the child was "old enough" has been rejected. Although that policy may have been followed with good intentions, many problems resulted. Many children would accidently learn from others they were adopted, instead of from their parents, creating confusion and parent-trust issues. Other children would wrongly assume their parents' silence was due to embarrassment about the adoption, creating shame in the child, unjustly believing something must be "wrong" with adoption.

Now, openness is embraced. Although your child grew in your heart and not physically in your body, you don't want to deny your young child the great joys every child receives when hearing about your anticipation of his or her arrival into the family, and how cherished and important a part of your family he or she has become. How your child views him or herself—and adoption itself—will depend almost exclusively upon you. This book will touch upon the most important issues for young children, and will reaffirm adoption was a decision made out of love by both you and the birth parent(s), all wanting one thing: a wonderful life for this child.

Adoption is a complicated subject in which even the most loving parent needs guidance. There are two excellent books which are truly critical for every parent: *Raising Adopted Children* and *Making Sense of Adoption,* both by Lois Melina. These books explore the many issues involved in adoption for your child (and you as a parent), in down-to-earth, helpful language. You will find yourself referring to these books for guidance again and again as your child moves from preschool, and into teens and adulthood. Because adoption books are rarely stocked by bookstores, these two books, as well as others for children like *Adoption Stories for Young Children,* are available for convenient and economical ordering by mail at the end of this book.

Hi. My name is Ryan.
I am 5 years old.

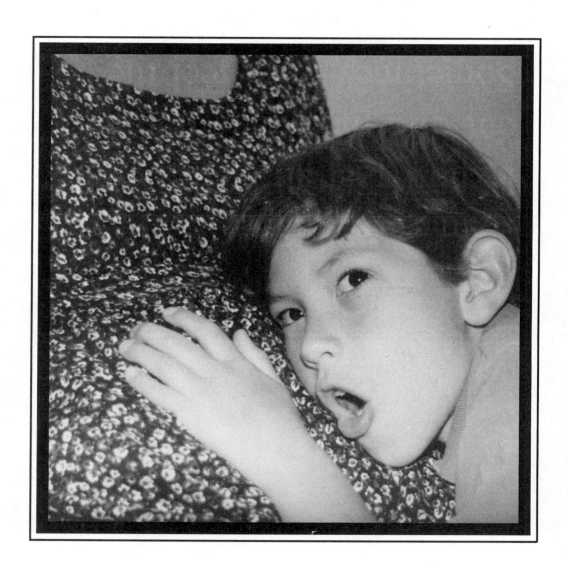

I am very smart.
I know that all babies come
out of a mommy's tummy.
Sometimes I can feel the
baby kick my hand! Wow!

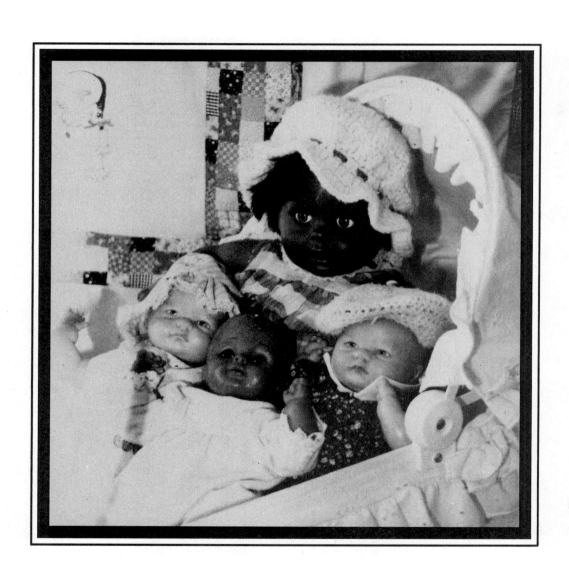

Some babies are boys.
Some babies are girls.
Babies are all different
colors—they can be white,
brown or black. All babies
are beautiful!

My babysitter's name is
Tammy. She lets me ride
my bike! She has a big
tummy because she is going
to have a baby.

Tammy is sad. She loves the baby very much, but she isn't ready to be a mommy. She still goes to school and she doesn't have a job like a mom and dad. She has no money for the baby's clothes and food and toys.

David and Lisa live next door to me. They are really nice. Their dogs are named Bosco and Shasta, and they pull me in my car real fast!

David and Lisa are sad
because they can't make
a baby in Lisa's tummy.

Surprise! Tammy had her baby and she chose David and Lisa to be the baby's mommy and daddy! Now David and Lisa are very, very happy.

David and Lisa named the
baby Brittany and they
adopted her. Adoption means
they will be her mom
and dad forever. That makes
Brittany very happy!

Tammy is doing great too. She wrote me a letter. She moved away and is going to college. She is growing up, just like me. She said she will always think of Brittany and is proud she made sure Brittany has the best mom and dad in the world.

Bosco and Shasta are happy
too! They are so happy
they had a doggie party!

I found a baby lizard in my backyard. I named him *Fingers*. He lost his mom and dad so my family sort of adopted him. That means we love him and he will be part of our family forever.

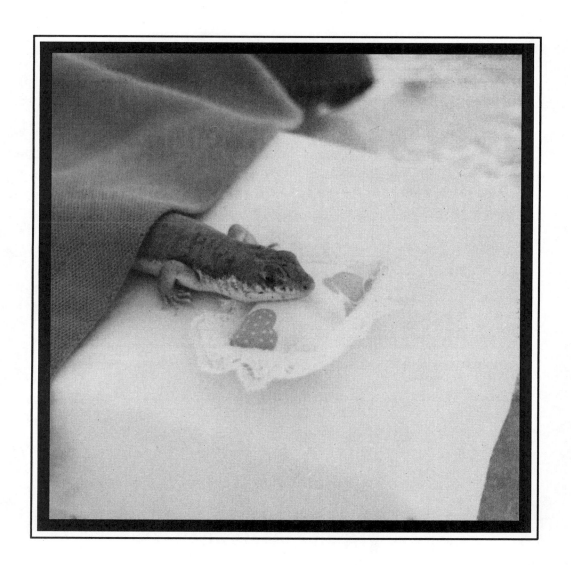

I tuck him in bed every night
and tell him a bedtime story,
like my mommy and daddy
do for me.

In the morning I send him to school in his school bus, just like my mom and dad send me.

I have a lot of friends who are adopted. This is Becky, my friend from church. She is adopted too. She likes to invite me over for tea parties in her playhouse. Yum, she gives me great cookies!

Today is Becky's Adoption Day. She gets a cake on her birthday **and** a cake on the day she was adopted. That's because they are both very special days. She sure is lucky! Two parties a year instead of one!

My very best friend is Mark. He was born in a country very far away. He came here to be adopted when he was 2 years old. We like to swing in his hammock!

My friend Andy lives down the street. He goes to a real fun preschool. There are a lot of fun things to do there, and he has a lot of friends.

Andy told his teacher he was adopted. And guess what? She told him that when she was a little girl she was adopted too!

When I go to the park I like to play with Gary and his sister Wendy. Gary and Wendy look a lot different, but were adopted by the same family. I know being a family doesn't mean looking alike. It means loving and taking care of each other.

My friend Suzie is adopted too. She lives on a farm with her mom and dad and grandma. I like to visit because we get to pick lemons and make real lemonade! Suzie's grandma is very smart. She says you spell adoption L-O-V-E.

Suggested Reading

Discussing adoption issues with your children is one of the most important subjects you will face. These issues begin when children are very young, and progress as they grow. Keep these books handy. They will quickly become your favorites!

■ *Tell Me Again About the Night I Was Born* by Jaimie Lee Curtis

This beautiful <u>hardcover</u> book authored by adoptive mother and actress, Jaimie Lee Curtis, has quickly become an adoption favorite.

■ *Through Moon and Stars and Night Skies* by Ann Turner

A colorfully illustrated book of a little boy who lives in a distant country and dreams of coming to live with his new adoptive family, then his dream comes true.

■ *Raising Adopted Children* by Lois Melina

<u>The</u> book for parents regarding the hows, whens and whys of discussing adoption with their children. The most popular book of its type in a decade!

■ *Making Sense of Adoption* by Lois Melina

Covers from "why did my birth mother place me for adoption," "am I different because I'm adopted" to "will you help me learn more about my birth parents?"

■ *Adoption Stories for Young Children* by Randall Hicks

Would you like another copy of this book for yourself or a friend?

■ *A Koala for Katie* by Jonathan London

A beautifully illustrated <u>hardcover</u> children's book. A young girl learns about the love involved in her own adoption by learning about the adoption of a baby koala.

■ *ADOPTING IN AMERICA: How To Adopt Within One Year* by Randall Hicks

The author of *Adoption Stories for Young Children* is also the author of the bestselling "how to" adoption book, *Adopting in America*. It details the pros and cons of twelve different types of adoption and tells you how to: spot red flags to a risky adoption; be selected quickly by a birth mother; select the best attorney or agency, etc. It also includes a valuable state-by-state review of each state's laws.

■ *The Open Adoption Experience* by Sharon Kaplan Roszia and Lois Melina

The newest book dealing with open adoptions, where there is continuing post-birth contact between the birth parent(s), adoptive parents and the child.

THESE BOOKS MAY BE ORDERED ON THE NEXT PAGE→

Book Order Form

Please rush the following books, indicated by a check in the box next to each title. I understand the price of each book **includes all packaging and postage costs.** Only California residents must pay sales tax. Books are normally shipped in 2 days.

☐ *Tell Me Again About the Night I Was Born* $15.95 (CA tax $1.16, total $17.11)

☐ *Through Moon and Stars and Night Skies* $7.95 (CA tax 62¢, total $8.57)

☐ *Raising Adopted Children* $13.95 (CA resident tax $1.00, total $14.95)

☐ *Making Sense of Adoption* $13.95 (CA resident tax $1.00, total $14.95)

☐ *Adoption Stories for Young Children* $9.95 (CA tax 77¢, total $10.72)

☐ *A Koala for Katie* $13.95 (CA tax $1.00, total $14.95)

☐ *Adopting in America* $16.95 (CA resident tax $1.23, total $18.18)

☐ *The Open Adoption Experience* $12.95 (CA tax 93¢, total $13.88)

ENTER TOTAL HERE (including CA sales tax if a CA resident): $_____
Please do not use cash or credit card. Make check payable to WordSlinger Press, P.O. Box 53, Sun City, CA 92586-9998; (909) 412-3788. Send order to:

_____
Name of purchaser

_____
Street number and address   City   State   Zip Code

Please provide your phone number if there is a problem in shipping: (_____)_____

Please note: If you are using the coupon to join the *Adoptive Parent Association of America*, for your convenience you may complete both sides of this page and mail both together. We look forward to serving you!

Free Membership Coupon
The Adoptive Parent Association of America

The purchaser of this book is entitled to one year free membership in the Adoptive Parent Association of America upon sending in a copy of the completed coupon and four postage-paid (33¢ stamp), self-addressed envelopes. Business-sized #10 envelopes are preferred but any size will be accepted.

The A.P.A.A. is a national membership organization of those who have adopted, or hope to do so. Members are provided a newsletter featuring articles by leading adoption experts concerning: new techniques toward adopting quickly and safely; changes in national and international adoption laws and trends; advice regarding discussing adoption issues with adopted children and reviews of new adoption books. Newly released adoption books are reviewed, and offered to readers. In sending in your envelope with the membership form and the required four envelopes, please be aware the normal postage required is 55¢.

── Membership Form ──
Please mail to: APAA, P.O. Box 53, Sun City, CA 92586

I am the purchaser of the book in which this coupon was included. I would like one year free membership in the Adoptive Parent Association of America. Enclosed with this completed membership form are four envelopes addressed to myself (preferably business-sized #10 envelopes but any size is accepted) with 33¢ postage affixed to each envelope.

_____

Your name(s)　　　Check one or both: ☐Adoptive parent(s); ☐Hoping to adopt

_____

Street number and address　　　City　　　State　　　Zip Code

Please list any adoption subject areas of special interest to you: